Figaro

Excitable and ready for adventure, Figaro knows
the neighbourhood like the back of his paw.

Pixie

Pixie has a nose for trouble
and a very active imagination!

Katsumi

Sleek and sophisticated,
Katsumi is quick to call Kitty
at the first sign of trouble.

For Jess, Nicola, Lisa and Gina, a big thank
you for making this book possible. - P.H.

For Jodie, my excellent agent and for Kate,
the finest bookseller in all the realms! - J.L.

OXFORD
UNIVERSITY PRESS

Great Clarendon Street, Oxford OX2 6DP

Oxford University Press is a department of the University of Oxford.
It furthers the University's objective of excellence in research, scholarship, and
education by publishing worldwide. Oxford is a registered trade mark of Oxford
University Press in the UK and in certain other countries

Text copyright © Paula Harrison 2021
Illustrations copyright © Jenny Løvlie 2021

The moral rights of the author/illustrator have been asserted
Database right Oxford University Press (maker)

First published 2021

British Library Cataloguing in Publication Data

Data available

ISBN: 978-0-19-277785-0

1 3 5 7 9 10 8 6 4 2

Printed in Great Britain by Bell and Bain Ltd, Glasgow

Paper used in the production of this book is a natural,
recyclable product made from wood grown in sustainable
forests.The manufacturing process conforms to
the environmentalregulations of the
country of origin.

Kitty

and the
Starlight Song

OXFORD
UNIVERSITY PRESS

Chapter 1

Kitty stared at the clock in the school hall, wishing the seconds would tick by faster. Her class were practicing their song for the end of term concert. Kitty loved the tune of *Dance Under the Stars,* but there was a

1

fluttering in her stomach. Their teacher had given each of them a line to sing as a solo. Kitty wasn't sure she wanted to sing all by herself.

The chorus ended and the solos began. Felix, on the front row, sang out clear and loud. Mrs Phillips, who was playing the piano, smiled at him and nodded. Kitty froze. It was nearly her turn. What if she got the tune wrong or forgot the words?

Mrs Phillips nodded to Kitty and played the next chord. Kitty opened her mouth and tried to sing, but no sound came out. She tried again but it felt as if the notes were stuck inside her. Some of the girls in the next row turned round to stare and Kitty's cheeks grew hot.

Mrs Phillips stopped playing with a tiny frown. 'Only two days to go, Kitty. You can do it, I know you can. Perhaps you could practice at home, in front of the mirror?'

Kitty nodded and her teacher turned back to the piano and started playing the chorus. Emily, Kitty's best friend, squeezed her hand. Kitty managed to smile but the fluttering in her stomach wouldn't go away. If she couldn't sing her solo in the rehearsal, how would she do it in the concert in front of all the parents and teachers?

Taking a deep breath, Kitty joined in with the chorus. She wished her heart would stop thumping so fast. She was used to feeling braver than this. She was a superhero-in-training after all!

Kitty had special cat-like superpowers that she used to help others. She had been on lots of exciting adventures in the moonlight with her cat crew. She could leap and balance as skillfully as a cat and she had super senses too. Seeing in the dark and hearing sounds from far away were really useful talents for a superhero. Best of all, Kitty could talk to animals and understand everything they said.

She loved being out in the moonlight, running along the rooftops. Performing in front of everyone was trickier than any of her night-time adventures. If only she could climb a tree or somersault over a chimney pot

instead of singing a solo!

* * *

After dinner that evening, Kitty sat down on her bed and thought about the school concert. The moon rose over the rooftops like a round white face and the city streets hummed with traffic.

Pumpkin, Kitty's little ginger cat, jumped on to the blanket and nuzzled her arm. 'What are you thinking about, Kitty?'

'I need to practice a song for the school concert and I'm nervous about my solo,' Kitty said, stroking his ears.

'But why? You're good at everything!' said Pumpkin loyally.

'Thanks, Pumpkin!' Kitty got up in front of the mirror and tried to sing, but she only managed two lines of the song before stopping again.

She could hear the words in her head:
When the stars are shining bright,
stretch your arms out to the sky . . . But
somehow they just wouldn't come out.

She gulped, remembering how her heart had thumped in the rehearsal. 'Maybe I'll practice later.'

Pumpkin looked disappointed. Then he pricked up his ears as a scratching noise came from the window.

Two cats were perched on the windowsill. One had a black-and-white coat and sleek black whiskers. The other was a tabby cat with honey-coloured fur and a long elegant tail.

'Figaro! Katsumi!' Kitty opened the window, beaming. 'I'm so glad to see you.'

Figaro bounded inside and smoothed his whiskers. 'It's wonderful to see you too! I have something extremely exciting to tell you. I bet you can't wait!'

Katsumi glanced at Kitty as she padded carefully through the window.

'Is everything all right, Kitty? You look a little tired.'

'Kitty's singing a solo in the school concert,' said Pumpkin.

'Ah, I see!' Katsumi nodded. 'That must be a little nerve-wracking.'

'Never mind about all that!' Figaro leapt from the window seat to Kitty's bed and prowled up and down. 'I've come with some very exciting news! You are ALL invited to my birthday party AND it's tomorrow night!'

Kitty's eyes lit up. 'Oh that really is exciting! How old will you be Figaro?'

'That's not really important,' Figaro said quickly. 'My kitten days are behind me but I

still know how to party!

I'll be serving the finest salmon, cod, and

halibut, and there will be decorations

all across my balcony. We can eat, drink,

and party under the stars. You will come,

won't you, Kitty?'

'I'd love to,' Kitty smiled. 'Thanks

for inviting me.'

'I'm so excited about it all that

I can't keep still!' Figaro pounced on

Kitty's pillow. 'Let's go outside and run

across the rooftops so I can use up some

14

of my energy.'

Kitty hesitated. She was supposed to be practicing her solo. The concert was only two days away!

'Come on, Kitty!' meowed Pumpkin. 'Let's go out and have fun.'

'A run in the moonlight might take your mind off things,' suggested Katsumi.

'I think you're right!' Kitty slipped on her trainers, put on her mask and cape, and climbed on to the windowsill.

The stars shimmered in the night sky and the moon poured silvery light over the streets below, making everything look magical. Climbing on to the rooftop, Kitty felt all her worries fade away. She loved being out here with the stars shining and the wind whooshing around the chimney pots.

Figaro bounded on to the roof, his tail held high. Katsumi and Pumpkin climbed after him.

Loud barking suddenly broke the silence. A sleek black cat climbed out of a nearby window with a shiny pearl necklace in her mouth. She leapt gracefully to the rooftop. Kitty recognized Dodger at once—the naughty cat she'd met on the night of the lantern parade.

A dog appeared at the window. 'Stop that thief!' he yelped, as Dodger made off across the rooftops.

'Quickly, everyone!' cried Figaro. 'We can't let the robber get away.'

Kitty's superpowers tingled through her body. Leaping from one roof to the next, she raced after Dodger with her cape flying out behind her.

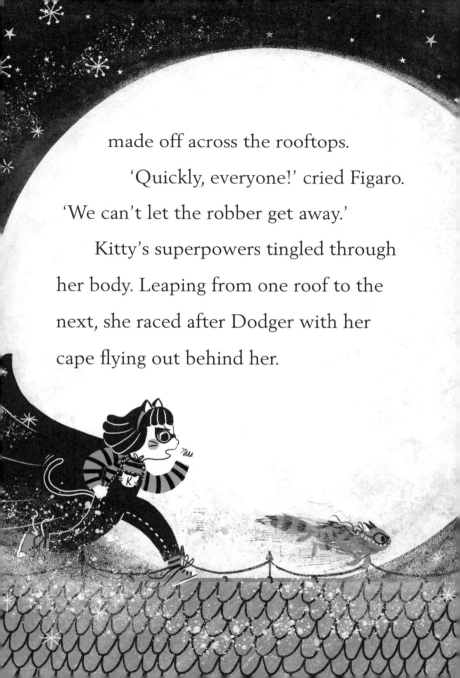

Chapter 2

Dodger turned to look at Kitty. Then the naughty cat smoothed her whiskers with a flick of her paw and gave a cheeky wink before running away across the rooftops.

'Dodger, come back!' called Kitty,

but Dodger kept on running.

'That cat is such a menace!'

snapped Figaro.

Kitty raced after Dodger with her cat crew behind her. Running along the roof, she somersaulted over a chimney pot. Dodger disappeared into the dark and, for a moment, Kitty thought she'd lost the cat thief. Then she spotted Dodger on the opposite side of the street, slipping over the wall into the park.

Kitty took a deep breath and used every bit of her superpowers. Leaping through the air, she grabbed hold of a nearby lamppost. Then she

slid gracefully down the long
post and landed on a high wall.
She crouched silently, listening
out for noises on the other side.

23

Figaro jumped to the top of the wall and peered down into the park. 'I'll catch her Kitty. I never let robbers get away!'

'Careful, Figaro! It's a long way down,' called Katsumi.

'Let's catch her together. We just need to be smart about it,' said Kitty.

But Figaro wasn't listening. 'Watch this, Kitty!' he cried, and crouching down on his haunches, he sprang into the air.

A gust of wind rocked the trees

just as he leapt from the wall. A branch whipped round and struck Figaro in the face as he fell. He gave a terrible yowl as he landed in the bushes.

'Figaro, are you OK?' Kitty leapt down beside him.

'OW! My eye hurts, Kitty!' Figaro
rolled around, clutching his eye with
one paw. His tail was bent over at a
strange angle.

'Oh no! Let me see.' Kitty knelt
down beside him.

Figaro mewed sadly. He tried to struggle to his feet before sinking on to the ground again. Kitty checked his face and ears before touching each of his paws. Lastly, she looked at his crooked tail. 'Does it hurt?' she asked him. 'Can you move it?'

'No, I can't feel it at all,' cried Figaro. 'My beautiful tail! It must be broken.'

'I'm sure it'll get better,' Kitty said soothingly. 'Come on, let's get you home.' Lifting Figaro gently in her arms,

she clambered back up
the wall.

As she turned to
go, Kitty saw a flicker of
movement in the trees.
She laid Figaro down, gently.
Dodger was balancing on a
narrow branch with the

pearl necklace
in her mouth.
She gave Kitty a
cheeky wave. Then, with
a twitch of her tail, she
disappeared into the
undergrowth.

* * *

Kitty and Pumpkin crossed the rooftops to see Figaro the next day. Kitty planned to look for Dodger and make her give the pearl necklace back, but she wanted to find out how her friend was first. They met Katsumi outside Figaro's house. Glittering stars grew brighter in the dark sky as they climbed up to Figaro's balcony together.

'I hope Figaro's feeling better,' said Kitty, tapping on the glass. 'It must be awful to be ill on your birthday.' She hid the present she'd brought along behind her back. It was a stripy black-and-gold bowtie, all wrapped up in shiny silver paper.

When Figaro didn't come to the door, Kitty pushed the handle and

stepped inside. The black-and-white cat
was lying in his bed with a white plastic
cone around his neck. His tail was
crooked and his eye still looked pink.

'Figaro!' gasped Kitty. 'How are
you feeling?'

'TERRIBLE!' Figaro meowed. 'My owners took me to the vet this morning and got me some eyedrops and some medicine for my poor tail. Then the vet made me put on this ridiculous THING that looks like a lampshade.'

'Why do you have to wear that?' Pumpkin stared at the cone.

'It's supposed to stop me scratching my eye . . . as if I would do such a thing!' Figaro snapped. 'I can't even groom my coat properly. This is the worst birthday EVER!'

'Poor you! I'm sorry you're not very well.' Kitty held his present carefully behind her back. It seemed the wrong time to give it to him. After all, he could hardly wear a bowtie at the same time as the cone.

'If only I hadn't chased that naughty Dodger!' Figaro groaned. 'And after all that, she still got away with the necklace.'

'Don't worry! I'm going to find her and make her give it back,' Kitty told him. 'We can still celebrate your birthday though. What about your party? You must be looking forward to that.'

'What time does it start?' asked Katsumi.

'It was meant to begin on the stroke of midnight, but there's no point having it now,' Figaro said with a sniff. 'My tail is MUCH too sore for me to run around getting everything ready!'

'I don't mind collecting the food and hanging up the decorations,' said Kitty. 'Come on, Figaro! Are you sure you don't want a birthday party?'

'Thank you, but I just don't feel like celebrating any more. I think I'll go to sleep till my birthday's over.' Figaro's whiskers drooped. He curled up in bed and rested his chin on his paws.

Kitty frowned a little. Figaro loved parties and he'd been so excited

about his birthday the day before. She was surprised to hear him say he didn't want a party. 'Bye then, Figaro. We'll let you get some sleep.' She slipped outside with Pumpkin and Katsumi.

'Bye, Kitty. No need to worry about me.' Figaro sighed heavily and closed his eyes.

Kitty hid Figaro's birthday present behind a potted plant in the corner of the balcony where she could find it later.

'Poor Figaro!' whispered Pumpkin. 'His birthday is completely ruined.'

'It doesn't have to be!' Kitty

murmured, closing the balcony door so

that Figaro didn't hear them. 'I think we

should fetch the party food, decorate

the balcony and invite lots of friends

to come at midnight. I think it would

really cheer him up!'

'That's a great idea!' Pumpkin
meowed.

'I think Figaro does want a
party really,' said Katsumi. 'But what
about the cone around his neck?

He seemed so embarrassed about it.'

Kitty thought for a moment. She understood why Figaro might not want everyone staring at his cone. She had felt awful in the rehearsal at school when everyone had looked at her. 'Maybe I could make him something to cover it.'

'And you should sing your song, Kitty! You know how much Figaro loves music,' mewed Pumpkin.

'Well, I haven't done much practice yet and there's so much else

to do!' Kitty said quickly. 'Why don't you go and invite all the neighbourhood cats? I'm sure Pixie and Hazel would come—they both like parties.'

'We could ask Cleo from the museum too,' said Pumpkin.

'I'll visit the sky garden and invite Diggory,' added Kitty. 'Also, I'll fetch the decorations and the party food. But first I'd better get that stolen necklace back from Dodger!'

'We'll bring as many friends as we can find,' said Katsumi. 'Shall we meet back here before midnight?'

Kitty nodded. Then she leapt on

to the roof, her cloak
swirling out in the wind.
'Let's make this an amazing
birthday for Figaro—one
that he'll never
forget!'

Chapter 3

Kitty climbed the drainpipe and darted along the rooftop. She knew exactly where to look for Dodger—the naughty cat that had stolen the pearl necklace. She lived in the Wonder Tower, which was the tallest building

in Hallam City. Kitty
stopped to gaze at
the gigantic tower
stretching up into
the night sky. It was
so tall it almost
seemed to touch
the stars.

Dodger lived in a restaurant on the top floor. She might be there now, eating the finest food and enjoying the best views of the city.

Kitty crossed two more rows of houses, before making her way to the ground. When she reached the tower, she went inside and pressed a button for the lift. The tower was hundreds of floors high—too far to climb even for a superhero!

The lift opened at the top floor. The name Cloud Restaurant was written

in gold letters above a magnificent set
of glass doors. People were eating inside
and there was a piano playing. The city
lay far below sprinkled with hundreds
of tiny streetlights.

Kitty crept through the doors and headed down a corridor. She remembered how much Dodger liked the restaurant's food. The cat thief was sure to be in the kitchen!

Chefs in white uniforms were

bustling around the ovens, chopping carrots and onions. Clouds of steam rose from the saucepans. A black cat was perched at the end of a worktop, drinking a smoothie through a long, stripy straw. A shiny pearl necklace hung around her neck.

Kitty leapt in front of Dodger, her hands on her hips. 'Hey, that necklace isn't yours! You should give it back right now.'

Dodger's eyes darted left and right as she looked for an escape. Then she gave up and took another slurp through her straw before wiping her whiskers. 'Hi, Kitty! This fish and mango smoothie's very tasty. Would you like some?'

'No, thank you.' Kitty held out her hand for the necklace.

Dodger hesitated for a moment before dropping the pearls into Kitty's palm. 'Fine then—have the silly necklace! It isn't really my style anyway.'

Kitty put the necklace carefully into the pocket of her dungarees. She sighed. Dodger had so much talent for climbing and acrobatics. It was a shame the naughty cat didn't use her skills for a good cause.

'How's your friend, by the way?'
Dodger stirred the smoothie with her
straw. 'That fall looked nasty.'

'Figaro's going to be OK,' Kitty
replied. 'Why don't you come to
his birthday party tonight,' she said
suddenly. 'I need another good climber
to help me decorate his balcony and
I think it's the least you can do, since
Figaro hurt himself trying to catch you.'

'I AM an excellent climber!'
Dodger grinned. 'I suppose I could
help, but I thought I might go on an

adventure tonight . . .'

'Don't you want to do something nice for another cat for once?' asked Kitty. 'You'd want everyone to come if it was your party.'

'I suppose so.' Dodger avoided Kitty's gaze.

'If everyone comes along it will really cheer Figaro up,' Kitty added. 'And there'll be salmon puffs and other nice things to eat.'

Dodger's ears pricked up at the mention of salmon puffs. She sprang

down from the
counter, her eyes
gleaming. 'Well,
I might be able to
come along and lend
a paw, but I'm not promising anything.'

Kitty left the Wonder Tower
feeling a little disappointed. She'd
thought for a moment that Dodger
would agree to come along and help.

She climbed up to the sky garden
to tell Diggory, the old cat that lived
there, all about Figaro's party.

The garden looked as beautiful as ever. An archway with white roses framed the entrance, and clusters of star flowers grew beside the bench. Kitty waited for a while, but Diggory didn't arrive. She left him a note

explaining about Figaro's birthday. Then she climbed back along the rooftops, frowning worriedly. She hoped Katsumi and Pumpkin were having more luck inviting cats to the party.

A cold gust of wind whooshed around the chimney pots. Kitty straightened her cat ears and made a gigantic leap to the next rooftop. She was determined to cheer Figaro up.

He'd helped her out on so many adventures. Now she could help him in return. She would take the pearl necklace back before getting everything ready for an amazing birthday party!

Kitty hurried home and slipped the pearl necklace through the window of the house two doors along. The dog inside dashed to the window, his tail wagging. 'Thanks, Kitty!' he barked. 'My owner loves that necklace. She'll be so happy to have it back again.'

Kitty waved and dashed back to the rooftop. The moon had climbed high in the night sky by the time she reached the fishmongers. Pickles, the tabby cat who lived there, gave her a parcel of salmon puffs, cod fingers and

halibut slices.

'I hope Figaro has a lovely birthday,' he meowed. 'I saved him the very best salmon puffs.'

'Thanks, Pickles!' Kitty beamed. 'You should come along later and join us!'

She hurried to the bakery next. Ludo, a friendly golden Labrador, was waiting for her with a basket. 'Here you are, Kitty! There are doughnuts and cupcakes in here, and Figaro's special birthday cake of course!'

Kitty peeked under the checked cloth covering the basket. Beneath the cupcakes was a large pink box tied with a red ribbon. Inside she found a fish-shaped birthday cake with glittery icing on the fins.

Kitty smiled. 'That looks amazing!

I can't wait for Figaro to see it. Thanks, Ludo.'

She waved goodbye and then checked her watch. There was only one hour to go until the party started and she still needed to find some decorations. She'd better hurry!

She skipped around the corner and turned into an alleyway lined with boxes and dustbins. She was so busy thinking about cakes and birthday banners, that she didn't notice the row of cats' ears poking above a cardboard box. A whiskery face peeked out of an orange crate and something knocked into a dustbin with a hollow thud.

Kitty turned around, but she couldn't see anyone. Maybe it had just been her imagination.

'YEE-OW!' A grey cat leapt out

from behind the bin with a huge yell.
He blocked Kitty's way, eying her
parcel of fish. 'Hi there, Kitty. Wotcha
doing in our alley?'

Chapter 4

Kitty recognized Duke, the plump cat with the long, droopy whiskers who had made such a mess of the sky garden last spring. His gang of cats scampered after him, all jostling and bumping into each other as they tried to keep up with their leader.

Kitty had forgotten that Duke and his band of alley cats often hung around this part of the city. 'Hello, Duke. You made me jump!' she said. 'What are you up to?'

'We were about to go searching for food.' Duke's eyes glinted. 'And then we smelt the fish in your parcel. Are those salmon puffs? Don't you think you should share them? We're VERY hungry.'

'I'm sorry—I can't!' said Kitty.
'They're for Figaro's party and
they're his favourite. If you promise
to behave, you can come along at
midnight and wish him a Happy
Birthday. Then you can have some
party food.'

'We don't want to wait till
midnight,' cried Duke. 'We want
them now!' And he pounced on
Kitty's parcel and pulled it out of her
hands.

'Stop it! That's for the party.'
Kitty reached for the package but
the alley cats jumped in, yowling and
tearing at the paper bag with their
claws.

Duke knocked the other cats
away. With a triumphant meow, he
dashed down the alley with the parcel

in his mouth. Kitty set her basket down and rushed after him. She couldn't let Duke steal the salmon puffs and ruin Figaro's birthday!

She raced down the alley, dodging dustbins and leaping over boxes. Duke reached the corner and turned to see if Kitty was following.

Suddenly, a black cat swung down from the roof and made a lunge for the parcel of fish.

Duke stared up in surprise. 'Huh, what's going on?' he mumbled.

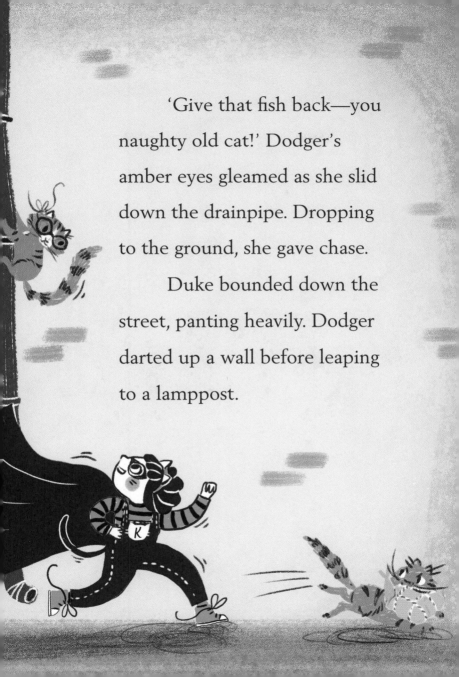

'Give that fish back—you naughty old cat!' Dodger's amber eyes gleamed as she slid down the drainpipe. Dropping to the ground, she gave chase.

Duke bounded down the street, panting heavily. Dodger darted up a wall before leaping to a lamppost.

She somersaulted gracefully over a postbox before landing right in front of Duke and snatching the parcel from his mouth.

Kitty swiftly caught up with them. 'Dodger, what are you doing here?'

'I'm catching this naughty thief for you!' Dodger gave Kitty the fish parcel. 'You can thank me now,' she added, twirling her whiskers.

'Thank you!' said Kitty, puzzled.

The gang of alley cats bounded up and stared at Dodger suspiciously.

'It's not fair!' Duke sank on to the pavement, still panting. 'I was only going to eat a little. I didn't think you'd really mind, Kitty.'

'It's really wrong of you to try

and steal Figaro's party food,' said Kitty, sternly.

A stripy ginger cat with a crooked tail edged towards Kitty, eyeing the parcel in her hands.

Dodger glared at the ginger cat until she sidled away again. 'Yes, it's very rude to steal someone's party food. I would never do that!' she sniffed and smoothed her whiskers.

'Sorry, Kitty!' Duke shifted on his paws, looking ashamed. 'Maybe we could come to the party after all.

We'd love to say Happy Birthday to Figgy-Roll.'

'It's Figaro!' said Kitty. 'You're welcome to come if you promise to be good. I want it to be a great party to cheer Figaro up. He's feeling sad after hurting his tail.'

'Will there be any music?' asked the ginger cat. 'I love a bit of singing and I can play the pipe too.'

'And I can play the dustbin drums,'
added a brown tabby.

Kitty's stomach flipped over as
she remembered that Pumpkin had
suggested singing to Figaro too. 'I guess
there ought to be some music. We
definitely need to sing Figaro Happy
Birthday! The party begins at midnight.'
She told them the address.

Duke and his band of cats padded
away down the street. Kitty turned to
thank Dodger for saving the fish, but
the black cat had vanished.

Kitty checked her watch again. She had less than an hour before the party started and she still needed to collect the party decorations and find a covering for Figaro's plastic cone.

She stared up at the sky, thinking hard. How could she make the cone look nicer? The stars glittered above her head like hundreds of beautiful diamonds. Seeing them sparked an idea in Kitty's mind. Figaro liked glitz and glamour, and he would love to sparkle like a star. Surely she had something at home that would turn him into the best-looking cat in Hallam City!

Kitty ran home and climbed through her bedroom window. She gathered the box of streamers from the cupboard under the stairs. Then she went back to her bedroom and pulled out her dressing-up costumes.

There was a pirate costume she'd worn to a party last year along with some hats and tiaras, but nothing seemed quite right for Figaro. She needed something bright and sparkly to

cheer him up and make him forget about
the plastic cone and his sore tail.

Kitty paced up and down her room.
In the distance, the city clock chimed
half past eleven. That meant she was
running out of time! She flipped head
over heels and landed on her bed.
Sometimes turning somersaults helped
her to think.

She ran to her wardrobe and took
out a red woolly scarf. It was plain and
ordinary, but if she added decorations she
could turn it into something wonderful!

Pulling out her make-and-do box,
she took out lots of jewels and
shiny stickers. She glued each
one very carefully to the
scarf. Then she added
feathers and bits of tinsel.
By the time she had
finished, the scarf
glittered with silver stars
and shiny paper.

Kitty smiled. She really
hoped Figaro liked it!

Gathering everything together, she clambered out of the window and raced along the rooftop. If she hurried, she could still get everything ready for the party on time!

Chapter 5

Kitty found Pumpkin and
Katsumi waiting for her in front of
Figaro's house. Pumpkin's whiskers
twitched nervously.

'Is something wrong?' asked Kitty,
looking at their faces.

'We invited lots of the cats from the neighborhood but no one has arrived yet and there's no light on in Figaro's room,' explained Katsumi. 'What shall we do if he's gone to sleep?'

Kitty looked up at Figaro's balcony. The room was dark and the curtains had been drawn. She pictured Figaro lying in the dark and feeling sad about his birthday. 'I bet he isn't asleep yet. Let's get everything ready and then we can knock on the window! He'll be so excited when he sees the decorations.'

Kitty climbed up to the balcony and began arranging the party food on the table. She set out the salmon puffs next to the doughnuts and put the birthday cake right in the middle.

Pumpkin untangled the streamers. 'This will look amazing!' he cried, holding up a golden Happy Birthday banner.

'Shhh, Pumpkin!' giggled Kitty, glancing at the balcony door.

Suddenly, a black cat dangled upside down from the drainpipe in front of her. Kitty jumped. Then she laughed as Dodger dropped gracefully on to the balcony and twirled her whiskers.

'You came after all!' said Kitty.

'I thought I deserved some food after rescuing the salmon puffs,' Dodger said cheekily. 'So, where shall I put these streamers?'

Kitty showed Dodger where she wanted the decorations to go. The black cat sprang nimbly on to the balcony railing with the streamers in her mouth. She hung from the edge of the roof by one paw to stick the Happy Birthday banner in place. Then she took some fairy lights from Katsumi and wound them round and round the drainpipe.

Jumping down again, she looked at her handiwork and grinned. 'There! Don't you think that looks amazing?'

'You've done a great job!' Kitty told her. 'Thanks for your help.'

'The food's ready too!' Pumpkin said, putting the last pack of cod rolls on the table.

Katsumi looked down at the street below. 'It must be nearly midnight. Pixie and Hazel said they'd be here by now but I can't see them.'

Kitty peered anxiously up and

down the shadowy street. Even with her super senses, she couldn't see any other cats. 'Maybe they're just a little late.'

'I hope they come soon,' meowed Pumpkin. 'Shall we wake up Figaro anyway?'

'I think we should wait,' said Kitty. 'Figaro will love it if there's a great big crowd ready to sing him Happy Birthday.'

So they waited.

The minutes ticked by. The

birthday banner flapped in the breeze and the fairy lights cast a twinkly glow across the balcony.

Kitty checked her watch. 'It's five past midnight,' she said at last. 'I don't think we can wait any longer. Let's wake Figaro and start the party.' She hid the special scarf she'd made for Figaro behind the potted plant with his birthday present. Then she tapped on the glass door.

There was no answer. Kitty peered through a chink in the curtains. Figaro was lying in his cat bed, but there was something about the twitch of his whiskers that made Kitty think he was still awake.

'Figaro?' she hissed. 'Are you asleep? I just wanted to say Happy Birthday!'

Figaro didn't move and Kitty wondered if he'd heard her. She knocked a second time but he still didn't get up.

Kitty rubbed her cheek worriedly. Maybe Figaro was too tired and unhappy to be cheered up by a party after all. For a moment, she thought about packing up the food and the streamers, and going back home.

'Maybe you could sing to him,' Pumpkin suggested. 'The song you're learning at school sounded lovely!'

Kitty hesitated and the words to *Dance Under the Stars* popped into her head. A fluttering

91

feeling grew inside her when she thought about singing. It's only Figaro, she reminded herself. There isn't a big audience that you have to sing to. She remembered how sad Figaro had looked earlier that evening. She really wanted to cheer him up!

Taking a deep breath, she began to sing:

'*When the stars light up the sky, take my hand and dance tonight . . .*' Her voice wobbled as she remembered how nervous she'd felt in the rehearsal at

school, but she kept going.
When she reached the chorus, she
sang a little louder. The night breeze
lifted her voice into the starry sky.
There was movement inside

and Figaro's whiskery face appeared at the window. His eyes lit up when he saw the balcony decorated with lights and shiny streamers.

'Kitty, this looks amazing!' he mewed, opening the balcony door.

Kitty went on singing as he stepped outside, his tail waving excitedly. When she reached the end of the song, Pumpkin, Katsumi, and Dodger all clapped their paws.

'Kitty, that was wonderful.

You've lifted my spirits enormously!' Figaro broke off, staring over Kitty's shoulder. 'Wait a minute! What's going on?'

HAPPY BIRTHDAY

Kitty heard mewing and rustling behind her. Dozens of cats were scampering down the moonlit street. More darted across the rooftops. They poured out of the nearby alley, running along benches and climbing trees. There were black cats and ginger ones, tortoiseshells and tabbies. Paw steps

pattered on the pavement and excited mewing drifted through the air.

'We did it!' whispered Pumpkin. 'Look, Kitty! Everyone's coming to the party.'

Kitty beamed. Figaro would have his perfect birthday party after all!

'What a lovely song!' called a ginger cat.

'Sing it again!' said a brown tabby.

Kitty's cheeks glowed. She hadn't realized there had been such a large audience.

Figaro wiped a tear from his eye. 'I can't believe you would do all this for me. Just look at the lovely streamers and all those wonderful salmon puffs!'

'We just wanted you to have a special party,' Kitty hugged him. 'Happy Birthday, Figaro!'

Chapter 6

One by one, the neighbourhood cats climbed up from the street. They crowded on to the balcony, clambering over chairs and balancing on the railing.

'But Kitty! How did you have time to organize all this?' Figaro asked, wide-eyed.

'Katsumi and Pumpkin helped me,' said Kitty. 'And Dodger hung up the decorations.'

'Look, here's Cleo from the museum,' mewed Pumpkin.

'And there's Pixie too!' Kitty waved to the fluffy white cat skipping along the rooftop.

'This is wonderful! But Kitty . . .' Figaro glanced down at the white cone around his neck. 'I don't have anything nice to wear!'

'Don't worry about that!' Kitty said quickly. 'I made you this . . .' She took out the special scarf that she'd hidden and draped it around Figaro's neck.

The jewels on the scarf gleamed in the moonlight and the shiny paper fluttered as Figaro turned his head from side to side. 'I love it,' he gasped. 'Kitty, you really are fantastic!'

The mewing and chattering grew

louder as more cats crowded on to the balcony.

'Hi Kitty! Happy birthday, Figaro!' Pixie pranced along the balcony railing. Hazel followed her, looking a little shy. Diggory, from the sky garden, padded slowly down the roof to join them.

'Hello, Pixie and Hazel. Hello, Diggory!' called Kitty. 'I'm so happy you came along.'

Cleo climbed on to the balcony followed by Duke and his alley cats. Duke sidled towards the table of party food, licking his whiskers.

'I'm glad you could make it,' Kitty told him.

'Very happy to be here!' Duke replied, helping himself to some cod fingers. 'Hey Kitty, maybe you could teach us that song you were singing.'

'Yes, please teach it to us!' cried his stripy ginger friend. 'I brought along my pipe to play some music.'

'All right then! We could all sing the song together.' Kitty clapped her hands for quiet. Then she taught them the tune of *Dance Under the Stars*.

When
she counted them in,
the cats' voices rose into
the air. Beautiful yowling
harmonies lifted over the
moonlit rooftops.

The alley cats sang too, with the stripy cat playing his pipe and a brown tabby banging on a dustbin lid. Duke tapped his paw to the rhythm and sang along in a deep purring voice.

Figaro tilted his head to one side, listening happily. Kitty's heart skipped. The tune sounded wonderful with everyone joining in and she didn't feel nervous at all!

'Thank you for the song, everyone,' called Figaro, when they finished.

'You look fantastic, Figaro,' said Pixie. 'Where did you get that scarf?'

'Kitty made it for me,' Figaro beamed.

'That reminds me! I got you something else too.' Kitty took out the present she'd hidden and handed it to Figaro. Pumpkin and Katsumi gave him little parcels too.

Figaro tore the wrapping paper off the presents. He loved Kitty's stripy bowtie. Pumpkin had brought him a shiny bell for his collar and Katsumi

gave him a pack of
tuna treats. 'I
thought this was
going to be a terrible
birthday,' he told them all.
'But it's been absolutely
splendid!'

Kitty smiled and patted his
shoulder. Then she carefully took the
fish-shaped birthday cake out of its pink
box. 'Ready everyone!' she called out.
'There's one more special song we need
to sing.'

They all sang Happy Birthday to Figaro and gave a yowling cheer at the end!

* * *

Kitty stood tall and straight at the school concert the following evening. She could see her mum and dad, and Max sitting in the audience and smiling at her. Her stomach flipped over as their teacher played the introduction to *Dance Under the Stars*. Kitty's best friend, Emily, squeezed her hand.

Kitty took a deep breath. Her stomach was full of flutters. Then she

spotted a pair of cat's eyes
gleaming at the window. Figaro was
watching from outside the school
hall, proudly wearing the special scarf
she'd made him.

You can do it, Kitty told herself.
You sang for Figaro once— imagine

you're singing just for
him, again.

The solos began and,
one by one, Kitty's classmates sang their
lines. When it came to Kitty's turn, she
shut her eyes for a second and imagined
she was standing on Figaro's balcony
under the stars. Then she sang loudly,
*'When the cold winds blow, dance and
twirl under the stars . . .'*

Then the chorus began and the
whole class joined in. At the end, the
audience clapped and cheered,

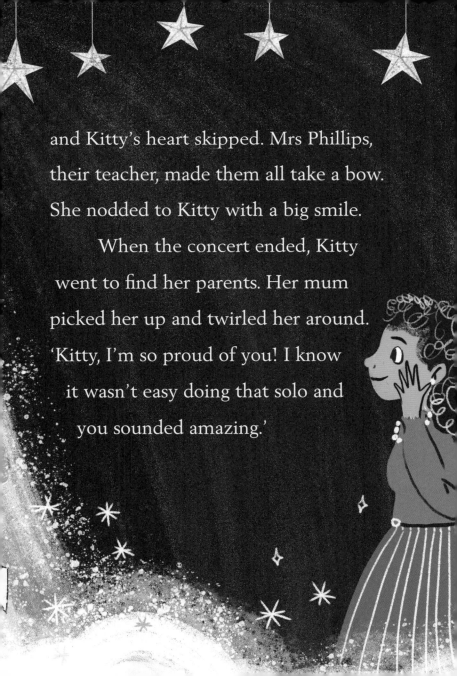

and Kitty's heart skipped. Mrs Phillips, their teacher, made them all take a bow. She nodded to Kitty with a big smile.

When the concert ended, Kitty went to find her parents. Her mum picked her up and twirled her around. 'Kitty, I'm so proud of you! I know it wasn't easy doing that solo and you sounded amazing.'

'Thanks, Mum.' Kitty's cheeks turned pink.

'We got you a present.' Mum gave her a tiny parcel. 'To remind you how brave you were to stand up and sing.'

Kitty tore off the paper and took out a glittery badge in the shape of a silver star. 'It's beautiful. Thank you!' She hugged her mum and dad.

'You could pin it to your cloak so it's with you every time you have an adventure,' said Mum.

Kitty touched the

shiny badge and smiled. She couldn't wait to show it to Figaro and all her cat friends tonight!

Super Facts About Cats

Super Speed

Have you ever seen a cat make a quick escape
from a dog? If so, you'll know that they can move
really fast—up to 30mph!

Super Hearing

Cats have an incredible sense of hearing
and can swivel their large ears to pinpoint
even the tiniest of sounds.

Super Reflexes

Have you ever heard the saying 'cats always
land on their feet'? People say this because
cats have amazing reflexes. If a cat is falling,
they can sense quickly how to move their
bodies into the right position to land safely.

Super Leaps

A cat can jump over eight feet high
in a single leap; this is due to its powerful
back leg muscles.

Super Vision

Cats have amazing night-time vision. Their
incredible ability to see in low light allows them
to hunt for prey when it's dark outside.

Super Smell

Cats have a very powerful sense of smell,
14 times stronger than a human's. Did you know
that the pattern of ridges on each cat's nose
is as unique as a human's fingerprint?

About the author

Paula Harrison

Before launching a successful writing career,
Paula was a Primary school teacher. Her years teaching
taught her what children like in stories and how
they respond to humour and suspense. She went on
to put her experience to good use, writing many
successful stories for young readers.

About the illustrator

Jenny Løvlie

Jenny is a Norwegian illustrator, designer,
creative, foodie, and bird enthusiast. She is fascinated
by the strong bond between humans and animals and
loves using bold colours and shapes in her work.

Love Kitty?
Why not try these too . . .

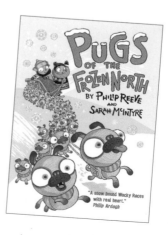